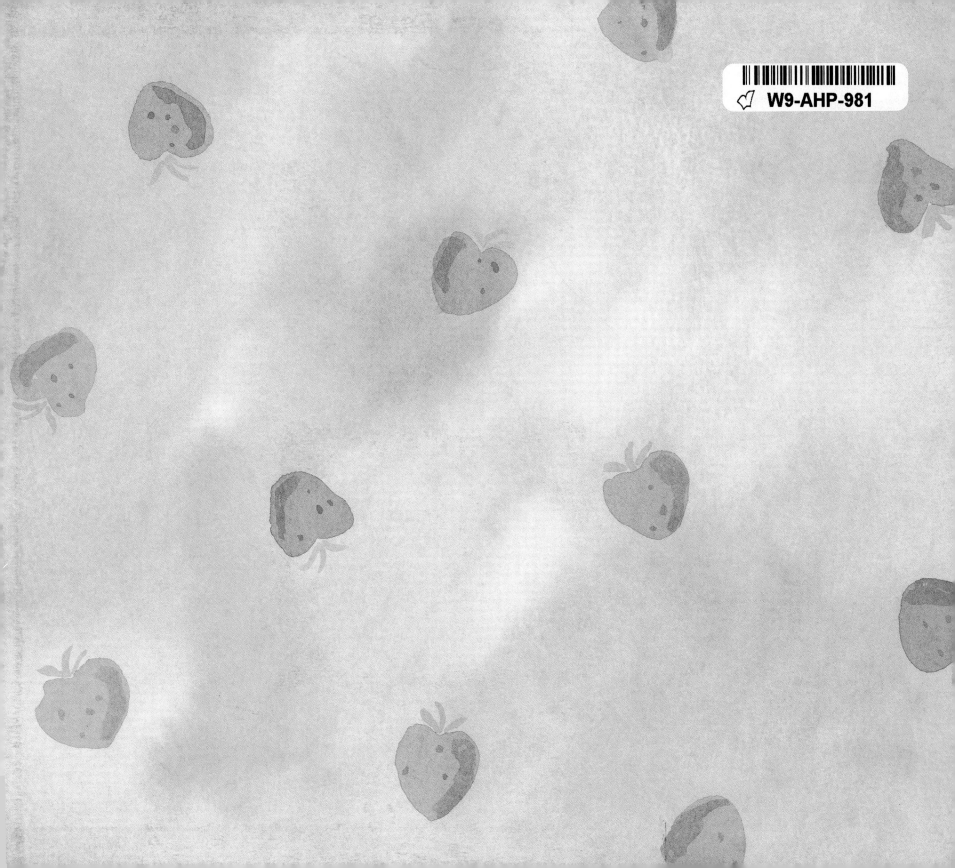

W9-AHP-981

For my good friend Elaine
−CF

For Grandma, with love
−JM

tiger tales
an imprint of ME Media, LLC
202 Old Ridgefield Road, Wilton, CT 06897
Published in the United States 2003
Originally published in Great Britain 2003 by Little Tiger Press
An imprint of Magi Publications
Text copyright ©2003 Claire Freedman
Illustrations copyright ©2003 Jane Massey
CIP data is available
ISBN 1-58925-032-X
Printed in Italy
All rights reserved
1 3 5 7 9 10 8 6 4 2

Night-Night, Emily!

DISCARD

by Claire Freedman

Illustrated by
Jane Massey

tiger tales

JP
FREEDMAN

It was bedtime, but Emily couldn't find her favorite bear, Mr. Teddy. She had looked everywhere.

Mommy tucked her in with Quackers
the Duck instead. "Night-night, Emily.
Good night Quackers," said Mommy.
"Night-night, Mommy and Quackers,"
said Emily.
"Quack, quack!" said Quackers.

Emily should have fallen fast asleep then, but she couldn't. The bed was too cold! *Oh no!*

Emily got up to look for Stripe the Cat.

"Night-night Quackers and Stripe," said Emily.

"Meow," said Stripe.

"Quack, quack," said Quackers.

Emily should have fallen asleep then, but she
still couldn't. The bed felt too empty. *Oh no!*
Emily climbed out of bed and found Hoots
the Owl.

"Night-night Quackers and Stripe and Hoots,"
said Emily.

"Hoo, hoo!" said Hoots.

"Meow," said Stripe.

"Quack, quack," said Quackers.

Emily should have fallen asleep then, but it was
impossible. The bed felt too hard. *Oh no!*
  Emily decided to look for Buttons
the Dog. She went downstairs and
found him behind the curtain.

"Night-night Buttons and Hoots and Stripe and Quackers," said Emily.

"Woof, woof," said Buttons.

"Hoo, hoo!" said Hoots.

"Meow," said Stripe.

Quackers didn't say anything. He had already fallen asleep!

Emily should have fallen asleep then,
too, but she felt wide awake now. The bed
covers were too loose. *Oh no!*

Emily got up to get Woolly Lamb.

"Night-night everybody," said Emily.
"Baaaaa!" said Woolly Lamb.
"Woof, woof," said Buttons.
"Hoo, hoo!" said Hoots.
"Meow," said Stripe.
"Quack, quack," said Quackers, who
had woken up with all the talking!

By now, Emily should have been fast asleep. But something still wasn't right with her bed. The pillow was all lumpy. *Oh no!*

"What's under here, making all these lumps?" said Emily.

She peeked under and found Mr. Teddy! "Oh, I was wondering where you'd gone! I looked all over for you!"

Emily put away
Quackers in the
toy box . . .

and she put Stripe
back on the shelf.

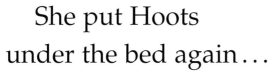

She put Hoots
under the bed again…

and Buttons and
Woolly Lamb went
back downstairs.

Emily and Mr. Teddy settled down under the warm, cozy covers. "Night-night, Mr. Teddy," said Emily.

"Grrr," said Mr. Teddy. And Emily fell asleep at last, because the bed felt just right.

Mr. Teddy should have fallen asleep then, too...

but suddenly the bed
was much too full!

JP
FREEDMAN   Freedman, Claire.

            Night-night, Emily!

S-3/12 LU-Never 6circs 16libs

Hiram Halle Memorial Library
Pound Ridge, New York